MR. MEN
LITTLE MISS
Save Christmas

Roger Hargreaves

Original concept by
Roger Hargreaves

Written and illustrated by
Adam Hargreaves

Little Miss Star loved Christmas trees.
Mr Greedy loved mince pies.
Mr Cool loved Christmas presents.
Little Miss Fun liked a Christmas party.
And Little Miss Tiny loved everything about Christmas.

Everyone liked Christmas.

Or did they?

There was one person I know who did not.

Mr Grumpy!

Mr Grumpy hated Christmas.

Tinsel sent him into a frenzy.

He could not bear the sound of carol singers.
He hated the sight of Christmas trees.
Christmas stockings sent him into a rage.
Christmas presents made him stamp his feet in fury.

Mr Grumpy hated Christmas so much that he even refused to believe in Father Christmas!

Father Christmas thought this was hilarious.

Ho! Ho! Ho!

Each year Mr Grumpy grew to hate Christmas a little bit more, until last year he just could not bear the thought of another Christmas.

So much so that he devised a plan to cancel Christmas.

Yes, you heard that right.

A PLAN TO CANCEL CHRISTMAS!

On the 1st of December, he opened all the doors on all the advent calendars.

Then he banged his drum so loudly no one could hear the carol singers.

He unscrewed all the bulbs in the Christmas lights.

He snipped off the ends of all the Christmas stockings.

And he chopped up all the Christmas trees.

He knocked all the berries off the holly.

He pulled all the 'bangs' in the crackers.

And he filled all the mince pies with toothpaste!

He unrolled all the sticky tape so that nobody could wrap a present.

And then, for good measure, he told everyone what their presents were!

He removed all the Christmas wreaths from everyone's front doors.

He released all the turkeys on Farmer Field's farm.

And, finally, he blocked up all the chimneys.
Just in case Father Christmas was real.

Christmas was cancelled!

After all his hard work, Mr Grumpy sat back in his chair in Gloom Cottage looking very pleased with himself. Suddenly, there was a knock at the door.

It was a very sad looking Little Miss Tiny. "Please, Mr Grumpy, won't you stop cancelling Christmas?" she pleaded. "Everyone is so unhappy. Even Mr Happy!" And a large tear rolled down her cheek.

"So what?" snapped Mr Grumpy.

"If you would only try a proper Christmas you would realise how wonderful it is," sniffed Little Miss Tiny.

"NO!" exclaimed Mr Grumpy. And he slammed the door in Little Miss Tiny's face!

But Little Miss Tiny was not one to give up. The next day she went round and knocked on Mr Grumpy's door again and pleaded her case.
And the next day.
And the next day.

And when she wasn't knocking on his door, she walked up and down outside his house chanting, "What do we want? Christmas!"
"When do we want it? Now!"

By the end of the week, Mr Grumpy was a lot grumpier, but he was also worn out.
And worn down.

"OK! OK!" he cried. "I will try Christmas. But! If I don't like it, then no more Christmases. Ever!"

Little Miss Tiny clapped her hands with glee and set about restoring Christmas.

Little Miss Neat screwed all the light bulbs back in.
Mr Messy's sticky fingers wrapped all the presents.
Little Miss Quick rounded up all the turkeys.
Mr Strong fetched a fresh batch of Christmas trees from the mountains.
Little Miss Busy baked new mince pies.
Little Miss Inventor knitted new stockings on her knitting machine.
Mr Rush rehung all the Christmas wreaths and holly.
And Mr Tall unblocked all the chimneys.

Christmas was back on!

Little Miss Tiny gathered all her friends for the most Christmassy lunch that you could ever imagine.

But what would Mr Grumpy think of it all?

He sat in the midst of the joyful gathering like a dark cloud in a sunny sky.

Little Miss Tiny nervously offered him a mince pie. He grudgingly put it in his mouth and chewed.

If truth be told, Mr Grumpy had never actually tried a mince pie, he had just assumed he would not like them.

He ate it all. And then had a second one.

Little Miss Tiny smiled to herself.

Then Mr Grumpy listened to a Christmas carol.
And, again, he had never actually listened to a
Christmas carol, he had always stuffed cotton wool
in his ears as soon as he heard the first note.
His foot began to tap along to the music.

He warily opened a Christmas present.
He had never opened a present before, he always
threw them in the bin. Unopened.
The glimmer of a smile appeared at the corner
of Mr Grumpy's mouth.

He gave a present.

And, of course this was something that Mr Grumpy
had never dreamed of doing in the past.

Little Miss Tiny thanked him so much that he smiled!

He pulled a cracker.
He wore a paper hat.
He read out a bad joke.
And laughed.

Mr Grumpy actually laughed!
Little Miss Tiny grinned.

To his surprise Mr Grumpy even enjoyed the company
and the laughter and the chatter. Mr Grumpy had
only ever been on his own at Christmas.

By the time Mr Grumpy tucked into the turkey and
trimmings, he was definitely what might be described
as jolly.

And he was positively beaming, as he gobbled up
his Christmas pudding.

Mr Grumpy was in such good spirits that after lunch he sat and admired the Christmas tree.

"Well I never," he said to Little Miss Tiny as the evening drew in. "I like Christmas!"

"I knew you would," said Little Miss Tiny. "And I have one more surprise."

There was a jingle of bells outside and then a knock at the door. "Mr Grumpy, meet Father Christmas!" cried Little Miss Tiny.

Mr Grumpy suspiciously eyed Father Christmas up and down. "Is that a real beard?" he said.
And then he tugged Father Christmas' beard!

"OW!" cried Father Christmas, whose beard, as you know full well …

… is as real as he is!